Wild Animal Kingdom

ANACONDAS

NICKI CLAUSEN-GRACE

BLACK RABBIT BOOKS

Bolt is published by Black Rabbit Books
P.O. Box 3263, Mankato, Minnesota, 56002.
www.blackrabbitbooks.com

Jennifer Besel, editor; Catherine Cates, interior designer; Grant Gould, cover designer; Omay Ayres, photo researcher

Library of Congress Cataloging-in-Publication Data
Names: Clausen-Grace, Nicki, author.
Title: Anacondas / by Nicki Clausen-Grace.
Description: Mankato, Minnesota : Black Rabbit Books, [2019] | Series: Bolt. Wild animal kingdom | Audience: Age 8-12. | Audience: Grade 4 to 6. |Includes bibliographical references and index.
Identifiers: LCCN 2017028385 (print) | LCCN 2017029479 (ebook) | ISBN 9781680725551 (ebook) | ISBN 9781680724394 (library binding) | ISBN 9781680727333 (paperback)
Subjects: LCSH: Anaconda—Juvenile literature.
Classification: LCC QL666.O63 (ebook) | LCC QL666.O63 C55 2018 (print) | DDC 597.96/7—dc23
LC record available at https://lccn.loc.gov/2017028385

Printed in China. 3/18

Image Credits

Alamy: André Gilden, 4–5; Mark Green, 32; petographer, 31; roberthard- ing, 14–15; en.wikipedia.org: D0ortegaven, 28 (t); Getty: Heidi & Hans-Juergen Koch/ Minden Pictures, 7; iStock: FernandoQuevedo, 1; Mark Kostich, Cover; Newscom: ANURUDDHA LOKUHAPUARACHCHI, 20 (snakes); Science Source: Francois Gohier, 10 (b); Martin Wendler, 10 (t); Shutter- stock: Alfmaler, 16 (silhouette); Anan Kaewkhammul, 24 (capybara); cellistka, 8–9, 24 (young), 26–27; Chonlawut, 20 (leaves); chronicler, 16–17 (bkgd); Colette3, 13; Dirk Ercken, 23 (frog); Ekaterina V. Borisova, 23 (fish); elitravo, 24 (ocelot); Fotos593, 27 (bkdg); Jannarong, 3; Johan_R, 24 (piranha); Lisa Strachan, 22; Odua Images, 24 (deer); Patrick K. Campbell, 28–29; reptiles4all, 24 (caiman); Superstock: Biosphoto, 19; NHPA, 24 (adult)
Every effort has been made to contact copyright holders for material reproduced in this book. Any omissions will be rectified in subsequent printings if notice is given to the publisher.

Contents

CHAPTER 1

A Day in the Life

A huge anaconda slides through the water in a jungle river. Its eyes peek above the surface. The snake heads for a deer at the water's edge. Without warning, the snake strikes. Dinner is served!

Hidden Hunters

Anacondas are large water snakes. Four kinds of anacondas live in the world. Their eyes and noses sit on top of their heads. These features allow their bodies to stay hidden in the water. **Prey** can't see them until it's too late.

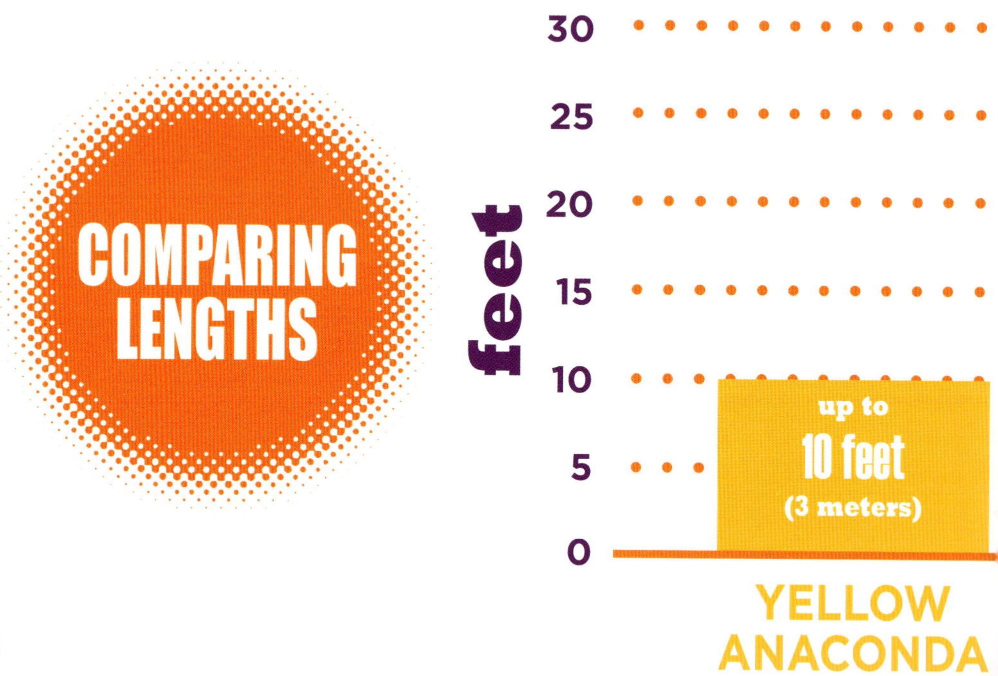

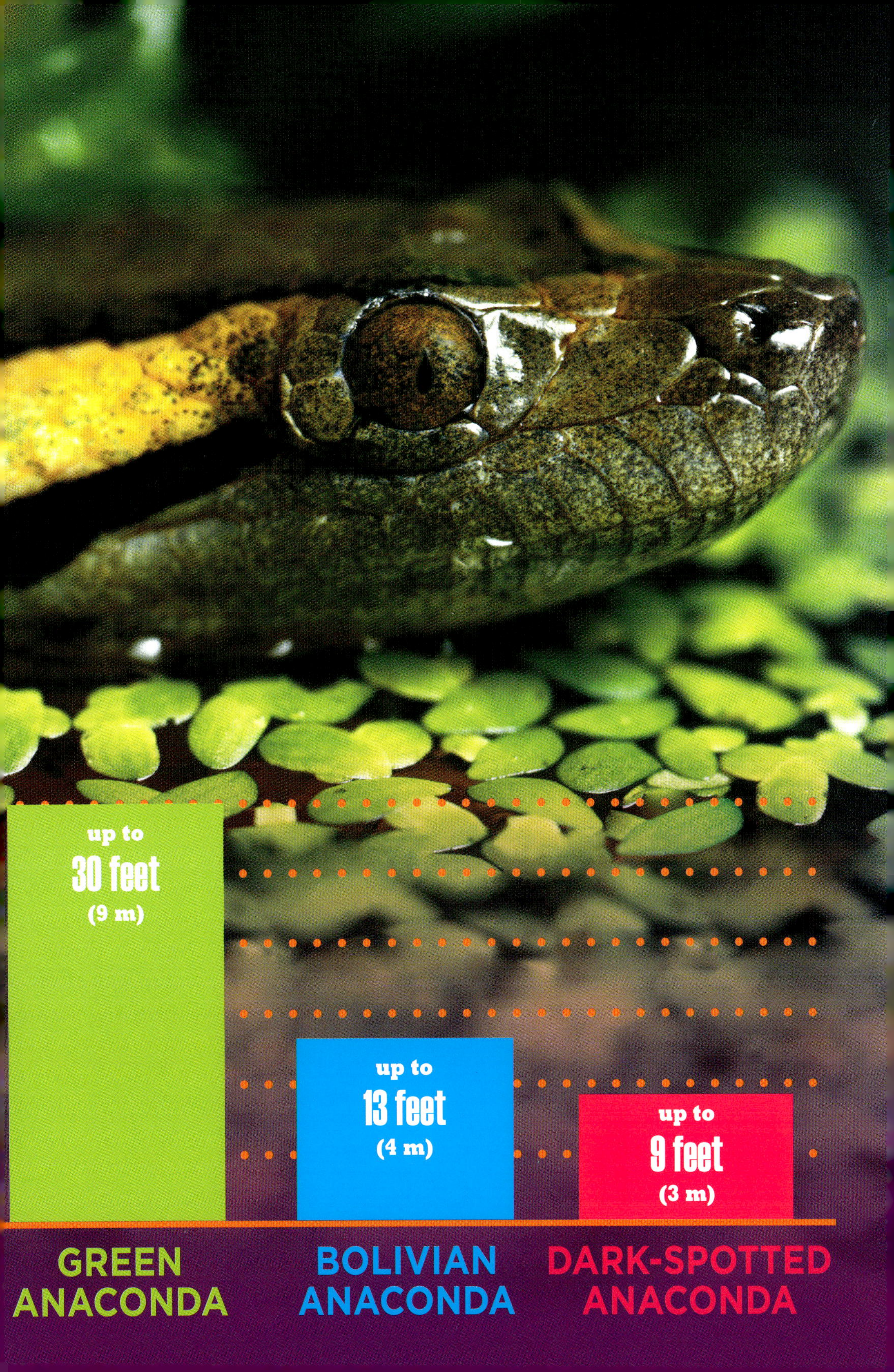

up to
30 feet
(9 m)
up to
13 feet
(4 m)
up to
9 feet
(3 m)
GREEN ANACONDA
BOLIVIAN ANACONDA
DARK-SPOTTED ANACONDA

ANACONDA FEATURES

DARK MARKINGS
NOSTRILS
MOUTH

Anacondas' jaws stretch really far apart. They can open wide enough to fit large prey. Stretchy skin lets their bodies hold such big meals.

CHAPTER 2

Food to Eat and a Place to Live

Anacondas are a kind of snake called **constrictors**. These snakes don't kill prey with poison. Instead, they squeeze prey. Then they swallow it whole.

Large meals give anacondas a lot of energy. These snakes can go weeks or months between meals.

Waiting for Dinner

Anacondas hide in the water, waiting for food. They catch animals from the riverbanks. They often eat deer, caimans, and capybaras. But they will eat almost anything they can get.

Water Snakes

Most anacondas live in South America. They like tropical swamps, wetlands, and streams. Anacondas spend almost all their time in the water. Sometimes they sun themselves on tree branches over the water.

Green anacondas are the heaviest snakes in the world. They weigh up to 550 pounds (249 kilograms).

WHERE ANACONDAS LIVE

Anaconda Range Map

CHAPTER 3

Family Life

Anacondas live alone most of the year. In spring, females leave **scent** trails for males. Many males form a ball around the female. They wrestle to get close to the female. The female might **mate** with several males.

COMPARING LITTER SIZES

dark-spotted anacondas

green anacondas

yellow anacondas

average number of babies in a litter

Babies

An anaconda mother keeps eggs in its body. After about seven months, it gives birth to up to about 80 babies. The babies are called **neonates**. After giving birth, the mother slithers away. Neonates are on their own.

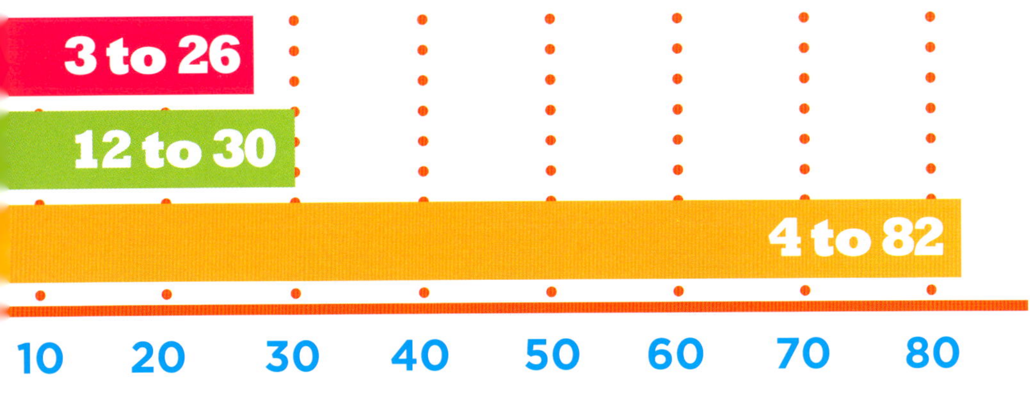

Early Life

As soon as they are born, neonates slide into the water. They hide from **predators** among water plants. They hunt for small prey.

Looking for Food

small fish

frogs

rodents

Anaconda Food Chain

This **food chain** shows what eats anacondas. It also shows what anacondas eat.

CHAPTER 4

Predators and Other Threats

Anacondas are at the top of the food chain. They still face **threats**, though. Baby anacondas are most at risk. On land, foxes, caimans, and ocelots hunt them. In water, piranhas and giant otters attack.

Anacondas can stay underwater for up to 10 minutes.

Human Threats

People kill many anacondas each year. Some people fear the snakes will attack. Others hunt the snakes for their skin.

These huge snakes are powerful creatures. They are an important part of the wild animal kingdom.

By the Numbers

0

NUMBER OF VERIFIED REPORTS OF GREEN ANACONDAS EATING PEOPLE

2002

YEAR THE BOLIVIAN ANACONDA WAS DISCOVERED

10 years
LIFE SPAN IN THE WILD

SPEED

ABOUT **5** MILES (8 KILOMETERS) PER HOUR **ON LAND**

ABOUT **10** MILES (16 KM) PER HOUR **IN WATER**

constrictor (kuhn-STRIK-tur)—a snake that coils around and squeezes prey

food chain (FOOD CHAYN)—a series of plants and animals in which each uses the next in the series as a food source

mate (MAYT)—to join together to produce young

neonate (NEE-uh-nayt)—a newborn human or animal

predator (PRED-uh-tuhr)—an animal that eats other animals

prey (PRAY)—an animal hunted or killed for food

scent (SENT)—a smell that is left by an animal or person

threat (THRET)—something that can do harm

verified (VEHR-uh-fyd)—confirmed or established as truth

LEARN MORE

BOOKS

Bell, Samantha. *Anaconda.* Exploring Our Rainforests. Ann Arbor, MI: Cherry Lake Publishing, 2015.

Gregory, Josh. *Anacondas.* Nature's Children. New York: Children's Press, 2016.

Smith, Molly. *Green Anaconda: The World's Heaviest Snake.* Supersized! New York: Bearport Publishing Company, Inc., 2017.

WEBSITES

Anaconda
kids.nationalgeographic.com/animals/anaconda/#anaconda-swimming.jpg

Anaconda
kids.sandiegozoo.org/animals/anaconda

Green Anaconda
www.nature.org/newsfeatures/specialfeatures/animals/reptiles/anaconda.xml

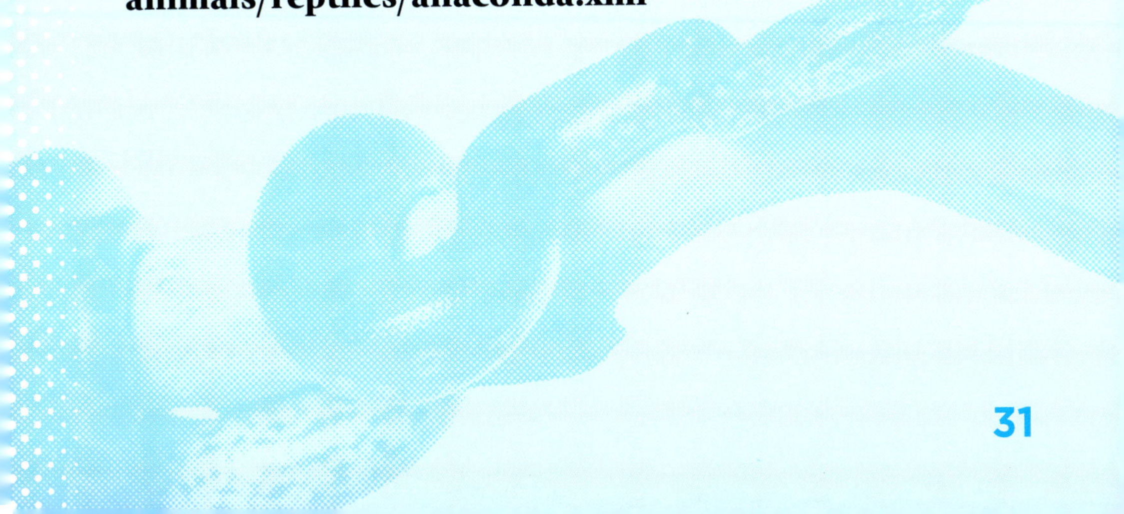

INDEX